Frenchie
the Bulldog
Fairy

Join the **Rainbow Magic Reading Challenge!**

Read the story and collect your fairy points to climb the
Reading Rainbow at the back of the book.

D0248196

ORCHARD BOOKS

First published in Great Britain in 2022 by The Watts Publishing Group

1 3 5 7 9 10 8 6 4 2

© 2022 Rainbow Magic Limited.
© 2022 HIT Entertainment Limited.
Illustrations © 2022 The Watts Publishing Group Limited.

HiT entertainment

A CIP catalogue record for this book is available from the British Library.

ISBN 978 1 40836 460 4

Printed and bound in Great Britain by Clays Ltd, Elcograf S.p.A

MIX
Paper from
responsible sources
FSC® C104740
www.fsc.org

The paper and board used in this book are made from wood from responsible sources.

Orchard Books
An imprint of Hachette Children's Group
Part of The Watts Publishing Group Limited
Carmelite House, 50 Victoria Embankment, London EC4Y 0DZ

An Hachette UK Company
www.hachette.co.uk
www.hachettechildrens.co.uk

Frenchie
the Bulldog
Fairy

By Daisy Meadows

ORCHARD

www.orchardseriesbooks.co.uk

Jack Frost's Ode

Puppy care sounds dull and dreary.
Training rules just make me weary.
These fairies must be made to see
No puppy matters more than me!

The fairies dared to tell me "no",
So far away their pups will go.
And if they don't do what I say,
I'll yell at them till they obey!

Contents

Chapter One: A Miraculous Machine   9

Chapter Two: Peaflower Moor   17

Chapter Three: A Giggly Game   27

Chapter Four: Pixie Pranks   37

Chapter Five: Goblin Seekers   49

Chapter Six: Fetch!   57

Chapter One
A Miraculous Machine

"I wish it would stop pouring," said Rachel Walker. "It would be much nicer for the animals if it was sunny."

Rain was drumming on the roof of the Leafy Lane Animal Shelter, where Rachel and her best friend Kirsty Tate were volunteering over half term.

They had offered to help care for some newborn puppies who didn't have a mother. This morning, they were busy cleaning the kennel while the puppies snoozed. The shelter manager, Nate, was playing with the older dogs in the rain.

"They don't mind a few drops of water," said Kirsty, looking out of the kennel window. "They're having fun."

"I'm glad we volunteered," said Rachel, sweeping the floor. "The puppies are gorgeous, and we wouldn't have met the Puppy Care Fairies if we hadn't come."

The day before, Li the Labrador Fairy had invited them to the Puppy Care Fair in Fairyland. While they were there, Jack Frost had stolen the fairies' puppies and their magical collars. He was angry that they wouldn't let him adopt a puppy without learning how to take care of it. Four of Jack Frost's goblins had taken the puppies and were training them for Jack Frost.

"I'm glad we managed to help Li," said Kirsty. "It's lovely to think that Buddy

and his magical collar are back where
they belong."

"But there are still three missing
puppies and collars," said Rachel. "Until
we find them, the fairies won't be able to
look after puppies around the world."

"We're going to find them," said Kirsty, covering the puppies with fresh blankets. "We won't let the fairies down."

The girls left the puppies fast asleep and took the dirty blankets and towels to the laundry room. Most of the washing machines were already full.

"Here's an empty one," said Rachel.

But before they could put the blankets and towels in, the machine started to spin by itself. The girls dropped their laundry and knelt down in front of it.

"Could it have been set to turn itself on at a certain time?" asked Kirsty.

"But there's nothing inside," said Rachel. "Or is there . . .?"

Slowly, a blur of sparkling rainbow colours appeared inside the machine. Then the machine door burst open. The

colours kept spinning as the sparkles
spelled out two words:

"One of the fairies needs us," said
Rachel at once.

"Fairyland, here we come," said Kirsty.

They opened the lockets that Queen Titania had given them. They were filled with just enough fairy dust to carry the girls to Fairyland. Without hesitating, Rachel and Kirsty sprinkled fairy dust over themselves. It gave them a warm, tickly feeling as they shrank to fairy size, with shimmering wings that lifted them into the air.

"Oh, something's pulling me," Rachel exclaimed.

"Me too," said Kirsty. "I think it's the rainbow whirl."

The shimmering colours were still spinning inside the machine, and now they were being pulled inside.

"This must be what it's like to be inside a tornado," said Rachel as the two friends were spun around in bubbles.

"A very colourful tornado," Kirsty
added, giggling.

They were on their way to Fairyland!

Chapter Two
Peaflower Moor

Seconds later, Rachel and Kirsty landed with a gentle bump. The sky was blue and the sun was shining. They were sitting on something soft and springy.

"It's moss," said Kirsty, gazing around. "I wonder whereabouts in Fairyland we've landed."

Rachel looked around too. It felt so good to be in Fairyland again! Bright yellow flowers on spiky shrubs stretched for miles around them.

"That's called gorse," said Rachel. "I've seen it before."

A few low, sturdy trees were dotted around, among patches of brightly coloured heather. Between the trees, Frenchie the Bulldog Fairy was sitting cross-legged on the moss, her head bowed down. She was wearing a blue frilled skirt decorated with pink flowers, an aqua-blue striped jumper and russet shoes. Her jet-black hair was plaited around her head in a coronet.

"Hello Frenchie," said Kirsty.

Frenchie sprang to her feet in surprise and delight.

"My message spell worked!" she exclaimed, hugging them both. "Thank you for coming!"

"It was a brilliant spell," said Rachel. "We loved the rainbow swirls and the glitter writing."

"We're happy to come and help you," Kirsty added. "But why do you need us?"

Frenchie took their hands in hers.

"After you and Li went to the human

world to find Buddy, the rest of us set off
to search Fairyland for the rest of the
puppies," she said. "I've been looking in
some of the most out-of-the-way places,
and at last I found a clue."

Rachel and Kirsty felt a tingle of
excitement.

"I found a trail of goblin and puppy
footprints," she said. "I'd know Pepper's
pawprints anywhere. It was her! So
I followed them all the way here to
Peaflower Moor."

"So that's what this place is called?"
Rachel asked. "We've never been here
before."

Frenchie nodded.

"The prints disappeared when I
reached the moss and gorse," she said.
"But I wasn't going to give up that

easily! I asked the moorland pixies who live here to help me, but they just giggled and said 'that would be telling'. Then I thought of you. If you could help Li to find Buddy, maybe you can help me to find Pepper."

"Of course we'll help," said Kirsty at once. "We'll do everything we can."

"But where do we start?" asked Rachel.

Just then, they heard giggles in the distance. Beside an outcrop of rock, six pixies were playing ball. They were wearing red caps, yellow trousers and green jackets.

"What colourful clothes they wear," said Kirsty.

"It's so that they can blend in on the moor," said Frenchie with a sweet smile. "The yellow gorse, the green moss and the red heather."

"Maybe we should try asking them again," said Rachel. "It sounds as if they might know something."

They watched as the pixies turned cartwheels around each other, throwing the ball with their feet.

"I don't think they're in a very helpful mood," said Frenchie.

"Pixies are a bit cheeky," said Kirsty thoughtfully. "I know they can be playful and stubborn. Maybe they just need to be asked a question in the right way."

Frenchie's face lit up with a huge smile.

"Pepper's like that too," she said. "When she's stubborn, I have to think of fun ways to persuade her to do the right

thing. Like getting her to eat healthy food instead of unhealthy treats."

"So how do you do that?" asked Rachel.

Frenchie thought for a moment.

"I have to make the healthy treats interesting and fun for her," she said.

"Then we have to do the same with the pixies," said Kirsty. "We have to make it interesting and fun for them to tell us what they know."

Rachel saw Kirsty's eyes sparkling.

"I know that look," she said. "You've got a plan, haven't you?"

Kirsty smiled.

"The pixies love to giggle," she said. "So let's give them something to laugh about. Maybe they'll give us some information in return."

Chapter Three
A Giggly Game

The three fairies fluttered over to the pixies.

"Hello," said Rachel. "This is Frenchie and Kirsty, and I'm Rachel. Peaflower Moor is so beautiful. Do you live here?"

"That's right," said the tallest pixie in a friendly voice.

"Lucky you," said Kirsty. "May we join in with your game?"

"The more the merrier," said another pixie. "We love to play!"

The fairies caught and threw the ball a few times. The pixies loved the game and chuckled as they tried different ways to

catch the ball — doing a headstand or in the middle of a backflip.

"I know how we could make the game even more fun," said Kirsty. "Every time one of us drops the ball, we have to tell you a joke."

"Great idea!" said the tallest pixie.

"What happens if we drop the ball?"

"Then you have to tell us something
you know about a goblin with a puppy
who was on this moor," said Kirsty.

"Are you sure that's what you want?"
asked a pixie with a curly white beard.
"Wouldn't you rather have a joke too?
We know some great ones."

"Thanks," said Kirsty. "But we'd rather
hear about the goblin."

The game started again. When the
ball came to Rachel, she dropped it on
purpose.

"Hee hee, tell us a joke," the pixies
giggled.

"What do you get when you cross a
sheepdog with a rose?" Rachel asked. "A
collie-flower!"

The pixies chuckled happily. Next,

Frenchie dropped the ball.

"What's a dog's favourite dessert?" she asked. "Pupcakes!"

The pixies giggled even more. Then one of them dropped the ball.

"I saw a goblin with a puppy," he said at once. "He was pulling it along on its lead, and it looked very tired."

"That's great news," said Kirsty. "It means the goblin was definitely here."

"And it means that Pepper has been walked too much," said Frenchie. "That's not so great. A puppy should only be walked five minutes for every month of its age."

The game began again, and next it was Kirsty who dropped the ball.

"Which dog breed loves bath time?" she asked. "A shampoodle!"

The pixies loved this one and kept repeating 'shampoodle' and bursting into fits of laughter. One of them missed the ball because he was giggling so much.

"Do you know where the goblin was going?" Frenchie asked.

"He was heading towards the Cracky Caves," said the pixie who had dropped the ball. "We play there sometimes when it rains."

"Would it be a good place for the goblin to hide with the puppy?" Rachel asked, curiously.

The pixies nodded enthusiastically.

"He might find a few pixie pranks if he wanders in there though," said the tallest goblin, spluttering with laughter.

The pixies agreed, nodding and giggling.

"We have to go home for our tea now," said the pixie with the white beard. "Thanks for the funny jokes."

"Which way should we go to find the Cracky Caves?" asked Kirsty.

The pixies all pointed over the brow of the hill.

"Thank you, it was lovely to meet you," said Frenchie.

The pixies waved goodbye and skipped away through the gorse.

"That was a great idea," said Frenchie, giving Kirsty a quick hug. "Let's go and find the Cracky Caves."

"It's a funny name," said Rachel as they flew off. "I wonder what makes the caves 'cracky'."

"Picking names is fun," said Frenchie. "I chose Pepper because she's small and fiery."

"She sounds like a handful, like my dog Buttons," said Rachel.

Frenchie laughed.

"She's a wonderful companion," she said. "She's friendly, funny and frisky, and she loves snuggling up on my lap as well as chasing balls – and bicycles. Oh my goodness, she even chased Bonnie the Bike-Riding Fairy once. Poor Bonnie!"

Rachel and Kirsty laughed, and then Kirsty saw a large outcrop of rock at the top of a steep hill.

"Look, it's got cracks all over it," said
Kirsty. "I suppose that explains the name."
As they flew closer, they saw one crack
that was bigger than all the others. They

fluttered a little way into it and heard a grumbling voice.

"Why do I have to look after a silly puppy?"

"That's the goblin," Frenchie whispered in excitement. "We've found them!"

Chapter Four
Pixie Pranks

The goblin was moaning and grumbling to himself deep inside the cave.

"Daft puppy won't even eat a bogmallow," said the goblin's voice, echoing around the stone walls. "But you've drooled on it so I can't eat it either. What do puppies eat anyway?"

There was a loud, snuffly snore.

"That's Pepper," Frenchie whispered. "She must be asleep after her long walk. I'm glad she didn't eat that bogmallow. They're very unhealthy for puppies . . . and for goblins."

"The goblin obviously doesn't know anything about that," said Kirsty.

"It's my job to help people keep their puppies healthy by making sure they eat the right food and get plenty of exercise," said Frenchie. "Pepper should be getting proper meals three times a day, not a few bogmallows in a cave."

"We'll get Pepper and her magical collar back," Rachel promised. "You have to be able to do your job."

The goblin groaned.

"I'm so achy," he muttered. "Where am

I supposed to sleep?"

They heard a loud *FLUMP* as the goblin flopped down, and then an even louder raspberry echoed around the cave.

"Argh!"

The fairies heard the goblin leap up again and stifled their giggles.

"That must be one of the pranks the pixies were talking about," said Kirsty. "A whoopee cushion."

Grumbling even more loudly, the goblin rustled around, trying to find another place to sit. Then there was a yell, and a giant rubber millipede came shooting out of the cave. It was followed by a flurry of rubber insects and a new batch of yells.

"Insects!" squawked the goblin. "I can't stand insects!"

He staggered to the entrance of the

cave, and the fairies scattered just in time. They ducked out of sight behind a tree. The goblin took off his cap and looked at a little silver lightning bolt badge that was pinned on top of it.

"Why shouldn't I rub it?" he asked grumpily. "I could be back inside the Ice Castle in ten seconds. That's what he said. Just enough magic for a trip to the Ice Castle for one goblin and one puppy."

"So why doesn't he go back?" Rachel whispered.

"Remember what Jack Frost said at the fair?" said Frenchie. "He has ordered the goblins to train the puppies for him. Then they will live in his castle so he can use their collar magic."

The goblin's shoulders slumped.

"Training puppies isn't fun," he muttered. "I don't even like dogs. I wish some of those stupid fairies would turn up. At least I'd have a reason to use the badge and get home."

Huddled behind the tree, the fairies exchanged worried looks.

"We can't get past the goblin without him seeing us," said Frenchie.

"And if he sees us, he'll panic and use

the lightning bolt badge to go back to
the Ice Castle with Pepper," said Kirsty.

"But he might not worry if we weren't
fairies," said Rachel. "What if we were
pixies instead?"

"Let's find out," said Frenchie.

She whispered the words of a spell.

"To fool the goblin's beady eyes,
A yellow, red and green disguise.
With twinkling eyes and bearded chin,
We'll make the goblin let us in!"

Then she waved her wand, and with
three faint pops, the fairies transformed
into three moorland pixies. They ran
towards the goblin, and he put his hands
on his hips.

"What do you want?" he demanded.

"Do you want to play a game?" asked Rachel.

"OK," said the goblin. "I'm bored of having only a puppy for company."

"Oh, I love puppies," said Kirsty. "Can we see it?"

The goblin stood aside and let them into the cave. They saw Pepper straight away. She was lying on the cold stone floor, curled up in a sleepy ball.

"Pepper," Frenchie whispered.

"What did you say?" said the goblin, darting her a suspicious look.

"Er, I said 'stepper'," said Frenchie, thinking fast. "It's a great game."

"Never heard of it," the goblin grumbled. "How do you play?"

Frenchie looked at Rachel and Kirsty in a panic.

"You have to step up on to something,"

said Kirsty. "Whoever steps up first is the winner."

Pepper snuffled in her sleep. Frenchie edged closer to her.

"Fine, I'll play," said the goblin, looking around. "Ready, steady, go!"

He leapt up on to a little ledge as Rachel and Kirsty pretended to scramble for a nearby boulder. He squawked in delight.

"I was first! I win!"

Frenchie had taken another step closer to Pepper.

"Let's play again," she said.

But the goblin shook his head.

"This is game is boring," he said. "Let's go outside and play hide and seek."

"Oh, but what about your puppy?" Rachel asked.

"She's boring too," said the goblin. "Go and hide outside."

"Maybe we could play inside," Rachel suggested.

The goblin scowled at her.

"Do you see any hiding places in here, peabrains?" he asked. "If you don't want to play then you can leave!"

The disguised fairies shared disappointed glances. They walked out of the cave as the goblin turned his back to them. Back behind the tree, Frenchie transformed them into fairies again.

Frenchie put her hands on her hips.

"I'm not going to be stopped by that grumpy goblin," she declared. "How are we going to get Pepper away from him?"

"This is hard," said Kirsty, frowning. "If he sees us, he'll just rub his badge and disappear with Pepper."

"Watch out," said Rachel suddenly.

The goblin had just walked out of the cave again, and this time Pepper was tucked under his arm.

Chapter Five
Goblin Seekers

"Taking care of you is the worst," the goblin was huffing to the little puppy. "Why do I have to do this? I could be eating bogmallows in Goblin Grotto. I could be having icicle swordfights in the Ice Castle. I could be catapulting slimeballs at toadstool houses. Instead I've got to live in a booby-trapped cave and look after a picky eater."

He stomped away from the cave and the fairies ducked behind the tree.

"If you won't eat bogmallows, what will you eat?" they heard him grumbling. "Berries? Leaves? Roots?"

"Those don't sound like very healthy choices for a puppy," said Rachel.

"Not really," Frenchie agreed. "And I bet that the goblin doesn't know which plants are safe and which are dangerous. You have to do lots of learning to be able to choose the safest wild foods."

The goblin trampled further away across the gorse, and Pepper looked droopy under his arm.

"She can't have had enough sleep," said Kirsty, worried.

"Puppies need plenty of rest," said Frenchie in an anxious voice. "Poor Pepper must be so tired and hungry."

Frenchie leaned back against the tree and rested her head on the bark.

"We're going to rescue her," Rachel promised, giving her a hug.

Kirsty peeped around the tree, waiting for the goblin to disappear over the brow of the hill. They couldn't risk him turning around and spotting them. Frenchie waited, tapping her foot, and Rachel absent-mindedly picked up a few pine cones that were scattered around on the ground.

"Maybe these would

make good playthings for the puppies at the Leafy Lane Animal Shelter," she said.

"Actually, pine cones aren't such a great toy," said Frenchie. "Pine oil can give dogs a poorly tummy, and some of them are allergic to pine sap."

She tapped each pine cone with her wand, and they turned into brightly coloured rubber sticks.

"They'll be perfect when the shelter puppies are a little older," she said.

"Thanks," said Rachel, smiling.

"The goblin's out of sight," said Kirsty suddenly. "Come on, and let's remember which way we go – it's really easy to get lost on a moor."

"Thank goodness we can fly," said Rachel. "If we do get lost, we can just fly up into the air and look down as if it's a real–life map."

They flew over the brow of the hill and paused, hovering while they looked for the goblin. They looked left and right, but all they could see was heather and gorse waving in the breeze. The goblin – and Pepper – had vanished.

"We should split up to search," said Frenchie. "I'll go left and you both go right. They can't have gone far."

Rachel and Kirsty zoomed across the moor, swooping as low as they dared. They scanned the yellow gorse and red heather for the green goblin, but at first they had no luck. Then Rachel heard bubbling, splashing and tinkling.

"It's a stream," she exclaimed, grabbing Kirsty's hand and pulling her towards the sound. "Let's look there."

As soon as they saw the stream, they saw the goblin. He was sitting on the bank, dangling his big feet into the water. Pepper was beside him, lapping up some water. Rachel and Kirsty ducked down behind a gorse bush and peeped out.

"What's he doing?" Kirsty whispered.

"He's looking at his cap again," said Rachel. "No, he's looking at the lightning badge. I think he's really longing to get back to the Ice Castle."

The goblin was so busy gazing at the badge that he wasn't paying attention to

Pepper. The puppy came closer to the gorse bush where Rachel and Kirsty were hiding. *Sniff! Sniff!* She was almost close enough to stroke.

"Pepper," Rachel whispered. "Pepper, come here, good girl."

Pepper paused, and then took a few steps back.

"She doesn't know our scent," said Kirsty. "How can we get her to come to us?"

"Frenchie said that Pepper likes to chase balls, remember?" said Rachel. "Maybe she likes to chase sticks too."

"But sticks can give dogs splinters and hurt their mouths," said Kirsty. Isn't there anything else we could use?"

Suddenly, Rachel remembered the pine cones that Frenchie had turned into rubber sticks. What had she done with them? She plunged her hands into her pockets and found the little sticks lying there.

"I've got just the thing," she said.

But just then, the goblin stood up.

"Dog!" he squawked, looking all around for Pepper. "Puppy! Come here!"

"Oh no, he's ready to move on," said Kirsty. "We have to keep him here until Frenchie finds us."

"You go and look for her," said Rachel. "I'll find a way to keep him here."

Kirsty zoomed away, and Rachel took a deep breath. It was all up to her now.

Chapter Six
Fetch!

Rachel threw one of the rubber sticks far away from the goblin. Delighted, Pepper bounded after it.

"There you are!" yelled the goblin, spotting her. "Come here, right now!"

Pepper took absolutely no notice.

Rachel put her hand over her mouth to

stifle a giggle as the goblin leapt after the puppy. She quickly threw another rubber stick in the opposite direction. Pepper scooted around, shot through the goblin's legs and jumped across the stream.

"Hey, stop that!" the goblin wailed.

He took a running leap at the stream but missed and landed in it with a loud *SPLASH*! Pepper stopped and looked at him. Her mouth was open and her tongue was hanging out. She looked exactly

as if she was chuckling, and the goblin
shook his fist at her.

"Don't you laugh at me, you pesky
pup!" he shouted.

He started to wade out of the stream.
Behind him, Rachel stood up and waved
another rubber stick in the air. Half crazy
with excitement, Pepper sprang back
across the stream, using the goblin's head
as a stepping stone. He went under the
water for a second time and came up
spluttering.

"You . . . you . . . dreadful dog!" he
squawked. "You puppy pest!"

Dripping wet, the goblin pulled himself
out of the stream and staggered towards
Pepper. She was lying down chewing
the latest rubber stick, but she stood up
when she saw the goblin coming. She

zigzagged left and right as he lunged at her.

"This isn't a game!" he wailed.

Rachel popped up from her hiding place for just long enough to send another rubber stick flying through the air. Pepper zoomed after it, yapping with joy. The goblin, sopping wet and with water weeds dangling over his left ear, stumbled after her.

"Stop right there!" the goblin panted as Pepper shook the rubber stick in her mouth, her ears flapping wildly.

He slowly reached his hand towards her red collar. Its silver tag, in the shape of a bone, flashed in the sunlight. Rachel scanned the sky, feeling desperate, but there was no sign of Frenchie or Kirsty. The goblin's bony fingers brushed the silver tag . . .

"*WOOF!*" Pepper dodged at the last second and started running around the goblin in circles. He spun on the spot, holding out his arms to try to catch her.

Round and round went Pepper.

Round and round went the goblin.

Then, groaning, he staggered sideways and dropped on to the moss with a bump.

"I feel sick," he wailed. "No one told me puppy training would make me feel this ill."

He clutched his head and found himself holding his cap. Slowly, he took it off his head and stared at it. Then he stared at Pepper.

"That's it," he said. "I'm wet, I'm hungry, I'm tired and I'm dizzy. I'm going to the Ice Castle and you can stay here to learn a lesson! When I come back later, you'll be ready to obey me!"

He rubbed the badge. There was a flash of blue lightning and the goblin disappeared.

"Yes!" shouted Rachel, leaping out from behind the gorse bush. "You clever, wonderful puppy, Pepper!"

"Rachel, I found her!" called Kirsty.

Frenchie and Kirsty landed beside
Rachel, and Pepper let out a yelp of joy.
Then she bounded
into Frenchie's
arms, licking her
eagerly.

"Oh Pepper,
I've missed you
so much," cried
Frenchie, burying
her face in the
puppy's soft coat.

"We should go,"
said Rachel. "The
goblin said he'd be
coming back."

Frenchie nodded

and flew straight upwards with Pepper safely in her arms. Rachel and Kirsty followed close behind, bubbling with happiness. They zoomed upwards through a fluffy white cloud, until they were hidden from view. Then they paused and hovered in the air.

"It doesn't seem enough to say 'thank you'," said Frenchie. "Without Pepper, I felt as if part of me was missing. Now she's back where she belongs, and I can make sure that puppies everywhere are eating healthily. You two have saved my best friend."

"That's all the thanks we need," said Kirsty, smiling.

They shared a hug, and then Frenchie tapped Rachel and Kirsty's lockets with her wand.

"There," she said. "I've refilled them with fairy dust ready for the next time you need them."

"Thank you," said Rachel. "We know there are still two puppies left to find, and we're ready to help."

"I'll tell Seren and Pandora," Frenchie promised. "But for now, I think the Leafy

Lane Animal Shelter needs you."

She waved her wand, and sparkling
fairy dust twisted out of the tip. It spun
the girls into a dazzling whirl, and then
they were falling forwards out of the
washing machine, back in the laundry
room at the animal shelter. Gasping, they
picked themselves up off the floor and
stared at each other.

"Washing machines are a very exciting
way to travel," said Rachel, panting and
laughing.

"I wonder how we'll get to Fairyland
next time," said Kirsty. "I hope it's soon.
I want to make the missing puppies as
happy as Pepper is."

"Me too," said Rachel, looking down
at the pile of dirty towels and blankets
they had dropped before they went to

Fairyland. "But first, we've got some washing to do!"

The End

Now it's time for Kirsty and
Rachel to help...

Seren the Sausage Dog Fairy

Read on for a sneak peek...

"I think this might actually be the best
shop in the world," said Kirsty Tate.

She turned slowly on the spot, smiling
at shelves lined with pet toys, collars and
leads; tanks teeming with jewel-bright
fish; and pens filled with fluffy rabbits
and guinea pigs. Her best friend, Rachel
Walker, ran her hand over a pile of soft
puppy bedding.

"Buttons loves it in here," she said.
"Most shops don't let dogs in, but here
they always make a fuss of him."

Kirsty darted over to a display of tiny

velvet cat collars.

"These would look so cute on Pearl,"
she said, running her fingers along the
row.

Rachel crouched down to look at some
dog treats. Then she shook her head and
stood up again.

"I could spend hours in here," she said.
"But we have to get on with our errand.
Nate is relying on us."

Nate was the manager of the Leafy
Lane Animal Shelter, where Rachel and
Kirsty were volunteering for a few days.
The shelter had rescued a litter of tiny
newborn puppies, and Nate needed
lots of help. He had given them a list of
things to buy from the pet shop. Kirsty
took it out of her pocket and read aloud.

"Five puppy collars," she said. "One

pack of puppy pads, one puppy comb, one pack of puppy milk formula—"

"Not so fast!" said Rachel, who was pushing the shopping trolley. "I'm still looking at the collars."

Kirsty giggled and came over to help pick five colourful collars for the white puppies at the shelter.

"Red, yellow, pink, green and blue," she said as she dropped them in to the trolley. "They'll look like a little rainbow."

Soon the trolley was filled with puppy supplies.

"And last of all, a jumbo pack of sanitising wipes," said Rachel, adding them to the pile. "Wow, our arms will be aching after carrying all this back to the shelter."

Just then, they heard a great

commotion. People were shouting, and dogs were barking and whining.

"What on earth is going on?" Kirsty asked.

They were near the back of the shop. When they walked to the end of the aisle, they saw a big archway with the words "Puppy Grooming Parlour" written in curly red letters. Under the arch were three uniformed puppy groomers, swarms of puppies and a crowd of owners. The groomers and the owners were all shouting and waving their arms around. And as for the puppies . . .

"Oh my goodness," said Kirsty, gasping.

There was a border collie whose silky coat had been curled into ringlets and decorated with at least a hundred red ribbons. A husky's coat had been gelled into spikes, and an unhappy-looking Pomeranian was modelling an 80s perm. There was a poodle whose curls had been straightened and an Afghan hound with a very wonky haircut.

"I'm so sorry," one of the groomers kept repeating. "I can't understand what's gone wrong today."

Rachel and Kirsty shared a worried glance. They knew exactly why the puppy grooming had been such a disaster. As well as volunteering at the shelter, they had been busy helping the Puppy Care Fairies. Naughty Jack Frost had stolen their puppies, as well as the enchanted collars that helped the fairies make their magic. The girls had helped to find Li the Labrador Fairy's puppy, Buddy, and Frenchie the Bulldog Fairy's puppy, Pepper, but two of the puppies were still missing.

"Until we find Wiggles and Cleo, everything to do with grooming and training will go wrong," said Rachel.

"Look at the state of my Japanese Akita," one woman wailed at the groomers. "He's gone blue!"

"I didn't want you to shave all her fur off!" a man was complaining, holding a Bichon Frisé wrapped in a blanket.

"I wish we could help," said Kirsty.

"There's nothing we can do right now," said Rachel. "Let's go and pay."

Feeling downcast, the girls walked along the toy aisle towards the tills. As they passed a large bucket of chew toys, Kirsty stopped in her tracks.

"What is it?" Rachel asked.

Kirsty pointed at the bucket.

"That squishy octopus is glowing," she whispered.

Rachel checked left and right, but there was no one else in the aisle. Her fingers tingled with excitement as she picked up the blue octopus.

"Do you think it's magic?" she asked.

As if to answer her question, the glow grew brighter and the toy disappeared. In its place was a tiny glimmering fairy.

"Hi, remember me?" the fairy said in a merry voice. "I'm Seren the Sausage Dog Fairy."

"Of course we do," said Rachel at once. "Welcome to Tippington."

Everything about Seren seemed bouncy and bright, from her green polka-flowered dress to her bobbed red hair. Her freckly nose scrunched up as she smiled at them.

"I'm so glad I found you," she exclaimed, jumping up and down on Rachel's hand and clapping her hands together. "I hoped and hoped that I'd find you in a quiet place so we could talk straight away."

"This isn't exactly quiet," said Kirsty, casting a nervous glance over her shoulder. "Shoppers could come down this aisle any minute."

"I'm sure they won't," said Seren.

She twirled over to a nearby shelf and landed on a rubber pig toy, which let out a loud OINK. Seren shot upwards again and squealed with laughter.

"Wiggles would love that!" she cried. "I have to get him one. When he comes home, that is."

She sat down and her smile faded a little.

"Is there still no sign of him?" asked Rachel.

"No one has seen him," said Seren. "But I heard a rumour, and that's why I'm here."

Read Seren the Sausage Dog Fairy to find out what adventures are in store for Kirsty and Rachel!

Calling all parents, carers and teachers!
The Rainbow Magic fairies are here to help
your child enter the magical world of reading.
Whatever reading stage they are at, there's
a Rainbow Magic book for everyone!
Here is Lydia the Reading Fairy's guide to
supporting your child's journey at all levels.

Starting Out

Our Rainbow Magic Beginner Readers are perfect for first-time readers who are just beginning to develop reading skills and confidence. Approved by teachers, they contain a full range of educational levelling, as well as lively full-colour illustrations.

1

Developing Readers

Rainbow Magic Early Readers contain longer stories and wider vocabulary for building stamina and growing confidence. These are adaptations of our most popular Rainbow Magic stories, specially developed for younger readers in conjunction with an Early Years reading consultant, with full-colour illustrations.

2

Going Solo

The Rainbow Magic chapter books – a mixture of series and one-off specials – contain accessible writing to encourage your child to venture into reading independently. These highly collectible and much-loved magical stories inspire a love of reading to last a lifetime.

3

www.orchardseriesbooks.co.uk

"Rainbow Magic got my daughter reading chapter books. Great sparkly covers, cute fairies and traditional stories full of magic that she found impossible to put down" – Mother of Edie (6 years)

"Florence LOVES the Rainbow Magic books. She really enjoys reading now" – Mother of Florence (6 years)

Read along the Reading Rainbow!

Well done – you have completed the book!

This book was worth 1 star.

See how far you have climbed on the Reading Rainbow opposite.
The more books you read, the more stars you can colour in
and the closer you will be to becoming a Royal Fairy!

Do you want to print your own Reading Rainbow?

1) Go to the Rainbow Magic website

2) Download and print out the poster

3) Colour in a star for every book you finish
and climb the Reading Rainbow

4) For every step up the rainbow,
you can download your very own certificate

There's all this and lots more at
orchardseriesbooks.co.uk

You'll find activities, stories, a special newsletter
AND you can search for the fairy with your name!